For Jean, Marion, Pierre, and Camille

Copyright © 1998 by Siphano, Montpellier. First American edition 2000 published by Orchard Books
First published in Great Britain in 1998 by Siphano Picture Books UK

Orchard Books, A Grolier Company, 95 Madison Avenue, New York, NY 10016

Manufactured in the United States of America. Printed and bound by Phoenix Color Corp.
Book design by Mina Greenstein. The text of this book is set in 17 point Bulmer MT.
The illustrations are watercolor. 10 9 8 7 6 5 4 3 2 1

Library of Congress Cataloging-in-Publication Data
Bassède, Francine. A day with the Bellyflops / by Francine Bassède.—1st American ed.   p.   cm.
Summary: On the first day she tries to work in her new office set up in the old toolshed, Mrs. Bellyflop is continually
interrupted by the antics of her three children.
ISBN 0-531-30242-3 (trade).—ISBN 0-531-33242-X (lib. bdg. : alk. paper)
[1. Pigs—Fiction.   2. Working mothers—Fiction.   3. Mother and child—Fiction.   4. Brothers and sisters—Fiction.]
I. Title. PZ7.B29285Dat 2000 [E]—dc21 99-27171

A Day with the Bellyflops

Francine Bassède

ORCHARD BOOKS • NEW YORK

Lilly, Peter, and Wiggly Bellyflop were very proud of Mother's new office in the old toolshed in the garden. They had helped to fix it up, and they had even given Mother their best drawings to hang on the walls.

"I only have two hours of work to do," said Mrs. Bellyflop. "If you play quietly and don't interrupt me, I will be finished soon."

"Afterward, can we make an apple pie?" asked Lilly.

"Why not?" said Mother.

Mrs. Bellyflop made herself comfortable in her office. It still smelled of freshly cut wood and paint.

Lilly slipped on her tutu and danced on the lawn, while Peter put Wiggly on the swing and gently pushed her.

They all looked as pretty as a picture.

Suddenly Lilly appeared at Mother's door with a scowl on her face.
"Peter and Wiggly messed up my tutu.

They are playing with the hose."

"The hose is only for the plants," Mrs. Bellyflop reminded them firmly as she dried Wiggly with a soft towel.

Mrs. Bellyflop had barely started working again when she heard loud footsteps outside the window.

Peter had eaten all the apples they had saved for the apple pie.
"I was hungry," he mumbled, his mouth full of apples.

Mother brought out the cookie tin and sat the children on the grass for a picnic.

But the picnic ended sooner than she expected. She hadn't even sat down when she saw four familiar ears passing by the window.

"What's all this mess?" she asked angrily.

"Wiggly dived into the mud and now there's mud all over us too," grumbled Peter and Lilly.

Mother gave them all a hot, soapy
bath, dried them off, and cleaned Lilly's
tutu and Peter's scooter.

"Now you must promise to play quietly!" said Mother. "I only have two hours of work to do and then we can all play together."

"We promise!" said Peter, Lilly, and Wiggly. They smiled sweetly and smelled very fresh and clean.

Lilly brought out her face paints. "Let's all be clowns," she suggested.
At last, some peace and quiet!

"Let's play circus," said Peter, jumping on Wiggly's tricycle.
"We'll be the acrobats," said Lilly as she and Wiggly took off on
Peter's scooter. "Here we go!"

"Now everybody hop on the scooter. I've seen that in the circus," said Peter.
"YAHOO!" they all cried. "YAHOO!" on the turn, and "YAHOO!" on the slope. Then . . .

SPLASH!
SPLASH!
SPLASH!

Three Bellyflops in the mud!
Mother heard the splashes from her office.

She didn't say anything. She simply grabbed
the hose and turned on the water.

"I thought the hose was for the plants . . . ," Peter
began, but Mother paid no attention. Without
uttering a word, she watered the piglets until
they were back to their bright pink piggy color.

At that moment, Mr. Bellyflop came back from
the market.

"Come and help me cook dinner," he said to the children. "Let's let Mother work."

But Mrs. Bellyflop found all kinds of excuses to stay in the kitchen . . .

just to be sure that things
didn't turn out like the last time
Mr. Bellyflop and the children
did the cooking.

It was late now. Daddy put Lilly, Peter, and Wiggly to bed, while Mother straightened up the house. Then he brought her a cup of tea and said, "You'll be able to work now, my dear."

Mrs. Bellyflop longed to go to bed herself, but she had to go back to her new office in the old toolshed in the garden.

She still had two hours of work to do!